Priscilla's
Perfect Tea Party

Written by
Jill Friestad-Tate

Illustrated by
Sue Houston Safianoff

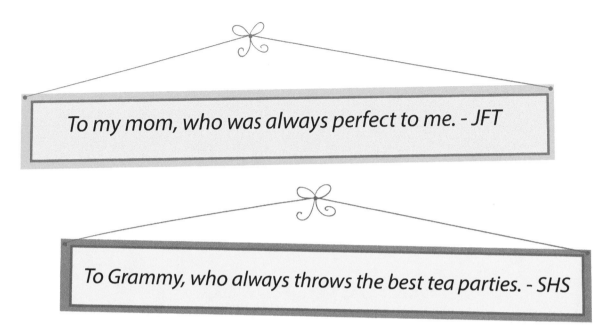

To my mom, who was always perfect to me. - JFT

To Grammy, who always throws the best tea parties. - SHS

Summary: Priscilla wants to have the perfect tea party for her Grandmother, but the harder she works to be perfect, the worse things get. Her brother, Bobby, helps her realize that perfection is not always what we imagine it to be.

Clear Fork Publishing
P.O. Box 870
102 S. Swenson
Stamford, Texas 79553
(325)773-5550
www.clearforkpublishing.com

Printed and Bound in the United States of America.

ISBN - 978-1-946101-48-8

Clear Fork Publishing

Priscilla **loves** lists. And she posts them *everywhere.*

There are lists in the **bathroom**,

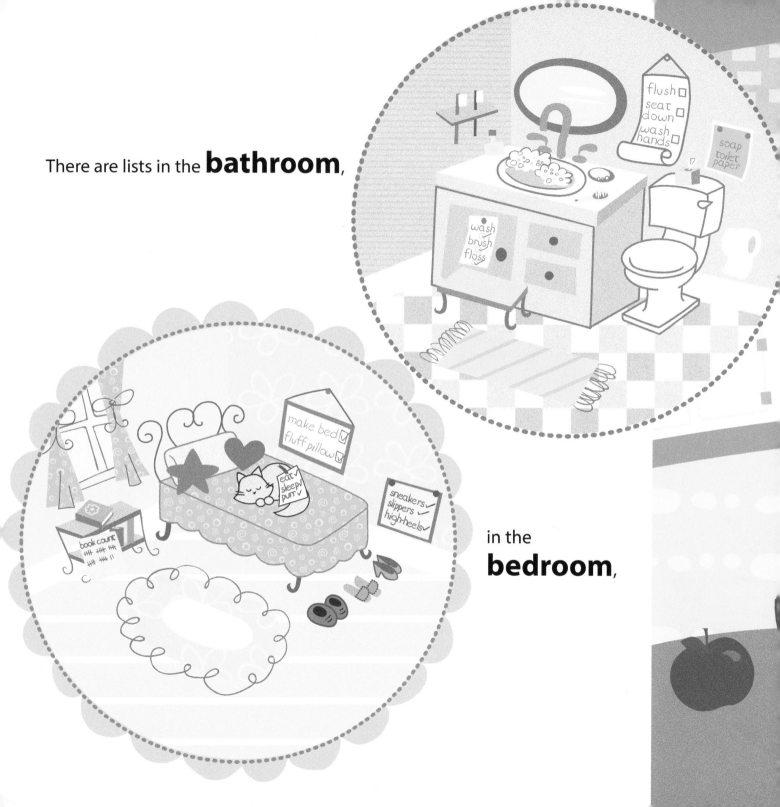

flush ☐
seat
down ☐
wash
hands ☐

soap
toilet
paper

wash
brush
floss

make bed ☑
fluff pillow ☑

eat ✓
sleep ✓
purr ✓

sneakers ✓
slippers ✓
high-heels ✓

book count

in the
bedroom,

and in the **kitchen**.

Today's list includes plans for a tea party.

"Grandma is coming from Florida, and everything must be **perfect!**" exclaims Priscilla.

While dressing, Priscilla reviews the list posted on the mirror.

"Lace dress… **check**.   High-heeled shoes… **check**.   Flowered hat… **check**.

Grandma's pearls and white gloves… **double-check!**"

Setting the table requires **another** list.

"Linen table cloth… **check**.

Fancy silverware… **check**.

Fine china with pretty pink roses… **chec**

Sugar cookies and jelly sandwiches…

double-check."

KNOCK-KNOCK-KNOCK

"Grandma can't be here **yet**. I'm not ready!" exclaims Priscilla.

January
February
March ✓
April ✓
May ✓
June
July
August
September
October
November
December

"Hey, Sis, can I come to the tea party?" asks Priscilla's brother, Bobby.

"You know I **love** sugar cookies and jelly sandwiches."

"Little brothers are not allowed—see the **list!**"

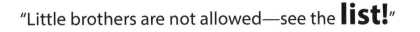

"Come on, Priscilla," begs Bobby. "I'll be the **perfect** gentleman!"

"You are noisy, dirty, and have awful manners.

Please leave so I can finish getting ready for the tea party," said Priscilla.

"Now, where was I?" Priscilla continues.

"Oh yes, forks on the left…**check**. Knives and spoons on the right… **double-check**."

ROAR! ROAR! ROAR!

"Oh, no! I'm not ready yet!" cries Priscilla.

"No, no, no, Tommy T-Rex, noisy guests are not allowed. At a tea party, you need to use an inside voice and act politely. Now, go away so I can finish getting ready!"

guest list
dress to impress
set table
sugar lumps
tea bell
beans

Tea List
earl grey
Peppermint
lemon tea
Jasmine
chamomile
oolong tea

Guest list
Grandma
Priscilla
Kiwi

earl grey
Jasmine
peppermint
lemon tea

linen table cloth
fancy silverware
fine china
sugar cookies

"All tea tastes sweeter with sugar. One lump or two?

Why, two is perfect, of course. **Check!**"

GRUNT GRUNT GRUNT

"Oh, no, Grandma is **here!**"

GRUNT

January ✓
February ✓
March ✓
April ✓
May ✓
June
July
August
September
October
November
December

"Not you, Pauley Pig—you look like you just took a mud bath. Dirty guests are not allowed! At a tea party, you must arrive squeaky clean and dress to impress. Now, **PLEASE**, go away so everything is perfect for my tea party."

"The golden tea bell will tell Grandma that it is time for the party to begin—

the perfect way to start. **Check!**"

BLURP-BLOINK-BLONK.

"**Finally**, Grandma has arrived!"

"NO, NO, NO! Space-Alien Sam, you do not know how to eat properly on Earth! At a tea party, you must use utensils and sip tea with one's pinky in the air. Now, go away so everything is perfect when Grandma arrives."

"Bobby, I told you—**no** dirty, noisy, or poorly mannered guests are allowed!" Priscilla shrieks.

"Well, look at **you**. How can you go to the party?" Bobby questions.

"Oh, no!" cries Priscilla,

"Everything was supposed to be perfect for Grandma's tea party!"

"I am everything a guest should **not** be—dirty, noisy, and using bad manners.
This was **not** on the list."

"But, Priscilla, **why** isn't it perfect?"
asks Bobby.

"Look around, Priscilla," says Bobby,

"you, me, friends, food—

everything we need for the perfect tea party.

Grandma's here, come on!"

ding
ding
ding

"Priscilla, would you like some tea?" asks Bobby.

"Everything is **perfect**, Priscilla, thank you!"
exclaims Grandma.

Jill Friestad-Tate
Author

Jill Friestad-Tate has loved writing since she was a child. As a business professor at a community college, writing continues to be a passion in her life. Always a kid at heart, she enjoys writing children's picture books and poetry about relationships and nonfiction topics. She is a member of SCBWI and has published several poems in Lyrical Iowa. She lives in Central Iowa with her husband and two boys and believes Iowa is the best place in the world to live.

Sue Safianoff
Illustrator

Sue is an illustrator and animator from Massachusetts. She started off her career as an artist for Carter's children's clothes. Later on, Sue branched off into 2d animation, drawing and animating e-cards and children's video games.
After learning computer animation, Sue animated on several feature films including 'Guardians of the Galaxy', and 'Arthur Christmas'.
Inspired by her book-loving toddler, she has returned to illustration with her focus now on children's books. She currently lives in Connecticut with her husband, son, and cat.